This dragon book belongs to:

....

Teach Your Dragon to Make Friends
My Dragon Books - Volume 16
Written by Steve Herman

Copyright © 2018 by Digital Golden Solutions LLC.
Published by DG Books Publishing, an imprint of Digital Golden Solutions
LLC.

Information contained within this book is for entertainment and education-
al purposes only. Although the author and publisher have made every
effort to ensure that the information in this book was correct at press
time, the author and publisher do not assume and hereby disclaim any li-
ability to any party for any loss, damage, or disruption caused by errors
or omissions, whether such errors or omissions result from negligence,
accident, or any other cause.

ISBN: 978-1948040433 (paperback)
ISBN: 978-1948040440 (hardcover)

www.MyDragonBooks.com

First Edition: August 2018

10 9 8 7 6 5 4 3 2 1

Then when he got the chance to play with other girls and boys, Diggory thought, "I'll have more fun, if I keep all the toys."

Diggory learned to argue;
he did it quite a lot –
If someone said, "It IS,"
he would say, "It's NOT!"

Sometimes Diggory Doo would brag about the things he'd done;
He'd strut around the neighborhood and say, "I'm Number ONE!"

Diggory whined, "I'm much too cold" or "Now, I'm way too hot." He was never satisfied with anything he got.

On a sunny day, he'd say,
"I wish that it were raining."
Soon Diggory Doo was all alone
because of his complaining.

Diggory said, "I'm different,
and that's the reason why
No one wants to be my friend."
Then he began to cry.

"Diggory Doo, you're wrong,"
I said, "and that is just a fact.
If you want to make some friends,
just change the way you act.

"Once you've met them, you can ask them, 'Would you like to play?' If you want to make new friends, this is the perfect way!"

"And whenever you are wrong,
don't insist that you are right!"

"Try to cheer a person up,
when you see he's feeling down."

Diggory cocked his head and said,
"I guess it's worth a try!"
So Diggory Doo took my advice,
and that's the reason why...

He now has lots and lots of friends.
He's learned a thing or two –
If you're a friend to others,
then they'll be friends with YOU!

Read more about Drew and Diggory Doo!

Visit
www.MyDragonBooks.com
for more!

Made in the USA
Middletown, DE
29 January 2023

23487849R00027